Geronimo Stilton
ENGLISH!

26 ON HOLIDAY 去度假

新雅文化事業有限公司
www.sunya.com.hk

Geronimo Stilton English
ON HOLIDAY　去度假

作　　者：Geronimo Stilton 謝利連摩·史提頓
譯　　者：申倩
責任編輯：王燕參
封面繪圖：Giuseppe Facciotto
插圖繪畫：Claudio Cernuschi, Andrea Denegri, Daria Cerchi
內文設計：Angela Ficarelli, Raffaella Picozzi
出　　版：新雅文化事業有限公司
　　　　　香港英皇道499號北角工業大廈18樓
　　　　　電話：（852）2138 7998
　　　　　傳真：（852）2597 4003
　　　　　網址：http://www.sunya.com.hk
　　　　　電郵：marketing@sunya.com.hk
發　　行：香港聯合書刊物流有限公司
　　　　　香港新界大埔汀麗路36號中華商務印刷大廈3字樓
　　　　　電話：（852）2150 2100　傳真：（852）2407 3062
　　　　　電郵：info@suplogistics.com.hk
印　　刷：C & C Offset Printing Co.,Ltd
　　　　　香港新界大埔汀麗路36號
版　　次：二○一二年七月初版
　　　　　10 9 8 7 6 5 4 3 2 1

ISBN: 978-962-08-5623-5
© 2008 Edizioni Piemme S.p.A., Via Tiziano 32 - 20145 Milano - Italia
International Rights © 2008 Atlantyca S.p.A. - via Leopardi, 8, Milano - Italy
© 2012 for this Work in Traditional Chinese language, Sun Ya Publications (HK) Ltd.
18/F, North Point Industrial Building, 499 King's Road, Hong Kong.
Published and printed in Hong Kong

CONTENTS
目 錄

BENJAMIN'S CLASSMATES 班哲文的老師和同學們 4

GERONIMO AND HIS FRIENDS 謝利連摩和他的家鼠朋友們 5

AN UNUSUAL HOLIDAY 一個獨特的假期 6

AT THE CAMPSITE 在營地上 8

WHAT FUN! 真好玩！ 10

　　A SONG FOR YOU! - Let's Go Camping!

THE SEASIDE HOLIDAY 到海邊度假 12

AT THE RESTAURANT 在餐廳裏 14

DO YOU REMEMBER? 你還記得嗎？ 16

A POSTCARD TO... 寄一張明信片給…… 18

　　A SONG FOR YOU! - A Postcard

A RELAXING TRAFFIC JAM 一次輕鬆的交通擠塞事件 20

TEST 小測驗 24

DICTIONARY 詞典  25

GERONIMO'S ISLAND 老鼠島地圖 30

EXERCISE BOOK 練習冊

ANSWERS 答案

BENJAMIN'S CLASSMATES
班哲文的老師和同學們

Maestra Topitilla
托比蒂拉·德·托比莉斯

Rarin
拉琳

Diego
迪哥

Rupa
露芭

Tui
杜爾

David
大衛

Sakura
櫻花

Mohamed
穆哈麥德

Tian Kai
田凱

Oliver
奧利佛

Milenko
米蘭哥

Trippo
特里普

Carmen
卡敏

Atina
阿提娜

Esmeralda
愛絲梅拉達

Pandora
潘朵拉

Takeshi
北野

Kuti
菊花

Benjamin
班哲文

Hsing
阿星

Laura
羅拉

Kiku
奇哥

Antonia
安東妮婭

Liza
麗莎

GERONIMO AND HIS FRIENDS
謝利連摩和他的家鼠朋友們

謝利連摩·史提頓 Geronimo Stilton
一個古怪的傢伙，簡直可以說是一隻笨拙的文化鼠。他是《鼠民公報》的總裁，正花盡心思改變報紙業的歷史。

菲·史提頓 Tea Stilton
謝利連摩的妹妹，她是《鼠民公報》的特派記者，同時也是一個運動愛好者。

班哲文·史提頓 Benjamin Stilton
謝利連摩的小侄兒，常被叔叔稱作「我的小乳酪」，是一隻感情豐富的小老鼠。

潘朵拉·華之鼠 Pandora Woz
柏蒂·活力鼠的姨甥女、班哲文最好的朋友，是一隻活潑開朗的小老鼠。

柏蒂·活力鼠 Patty Spring
美麗迷人的電視新聞工作者，致力於她熱愛的電視事業。

賴皮 Trappola
謝利連摩的表弟，非常喜歡食物，風趣幽默，是一隻饞嘴、愛開玩笑的老鼠，善於將歡樂傳遞給每一隻鼠。

麗萍姑媽 Zia Lippa
謝利連摩的姑媽，對鼠十分友善，又和藹可親，只想將最好的給身邊的鼠。

艾拿 Iena
謝利連摩的好朋友，充滿活力，熱愛各項運動，他希望能把對運動的熱誠傳給謝利連摩。

史奎克·愛管閒事鼠 Ficcanaso Squitt
謝利連摩的好朋友，是一個非常有頭腦的私家偵探，總是穿著一件黃色的乾濕樓。

AN UNUSUAL HOLIDAY
一個獨特的假期

親愛的小朋友，我的朋友柏蒂·活力鼠邀請我和我的侄兒班哲文，還有她的姨甥女潘朵拉一起去度假，這個主意多好啊！可惜他們選了去露營……你們很了解我的，是不是？我很有智慧，非常有智慧，但我對搭帳篷可不在行！現在就要出發了，我決不能臨陣退縮……你們也一起來吧，說不定有意想不到的經歷呢！

We packed our bags.
我們收拾好行裝。

跟我謝利連摩‧史提頓一起學英文，
就像玩遊戲一樣簡單好玩！

你可以一邊看着圖畫一邊讀。
以下有幾個標誌，你要特別留意：

當看到 标誌時，你可以聽CD，
一邊聽，一邊跟着朗讀，還可以跟
着一起唱歌。

當看到 ★ 標誌時，你可以和朋友
們一起玩遊戲，或者嘗試回答問
題。題目很簡單，它們對鞏固你所
學過的內容很有幫助。

當看到 標誌時，你要注意看一
下格子裏的生字，反覆唸幾遍，掌
握發音。

最後，不要忘記完成小測驗和練習
冊裏的問題！看看你有多聰明吧。

祝大家學得開開心心！

謝利連摩‧史提頓

AT THE CAMPSITE
在營地上

　　抵達營地後，第一件要做的事當然就是搭帳篷了，可是我卻不知道該從哪裏入手，幸好柏蒂和兩個孩子很快就把帳篷搭好了。露營所需的物品真多呢，有睡袋、手電筒、露營專用煮食爐、牀墊⋯⋯你知道這些物品用英語該怎麼說嗎？跟我一起說說看吧。

★ 試用英語說出：「我們一起來搭帳篷吧！」

答案：*Let's pitch the tent!*

柏蒂回想起她小時候也來過這裏露營，當時導師還跟他們玩尋寶遊戲呢。最後，當然是柏蒂那組找到了寶藏啦。

When I was a little girl, I used to come here to camp.

I remember our group leader organised a treasure hunt once.

We started to look for the clues.

In the end we found the treasure!

Well... what was it?

And where was it?

look for 找尋
in the end 最後

It was a pile of comics hidden under our group leader's mattress!

9

WHAT FUN! 真好玩！

班哲文和潘朵拉很喜歡露營，因為我們除了可以在營地玩各種不同的活動外，還可以在河邊散步，在樹林裏遠足，在草地上野餐……

Patty organises a trip to the river.

Pandora suggests a walk in the woods.

They organise a really nice picnic, but...

! break out　突然發生
go back　回去

... a storm breaks out and everybody has to go back to the campsite!

可是，那天晚上我睡得不好，因為我不習慣睡在帳篷裏。於是第二天吃早餐時，我提議到海邊度假，讓大家可以住在酒店裏。

I woke up at five.
我五點鐘起牀。

 A SONG FOR YOU! Track 1

Let's Go Camping!

It's nice camping
with my friends
and my parents when
the summer comes!
Sleeping in a tent,
going on a treasure hunt,

having a barbecue
and losing track of time!
Camping is beautiful
and makes me feel happy!
Camping is beautiful,
let's go camping!

THE SEASIDE HOLIDAY
到海邊度假

　　我預訂的酒店就在鼠爪灣海濱旁。這裏除了有不同類型的房間外，還有遊戲室、健身室、游泳池、餐廳等，設備十分齊全。班哲文和潘朵拉已急不及待要到遊戲室去玩了。

room with the sea view
海景套房

single room
單人房

twin room
有兩張單人牀的雙人房

double room
有一張雙人牀的雙人房

bathroom 浴室

reception 接待處

information desk 詢問處

lift 升降機

porter 雜工

waiter 侍應

waitress 女侍應

Here are the keys to the rooms.

Thank you!

Number 105 is on the first floor; number 208 is on the second floor.

Here are the keys.
這是鎖匙。

12

AT THE RESTAURANT
在餐廳裏

賴皮也在放假，於是他決定來鼠爪灣找我們。我們在酒店的餐廳裏一起吃午餐。賴皮打開餐牌一看，上面的菜式多得令他眼花繚亂，他真的想點齊每一道菜。

吃飯的時候，柏蒂教班哲文和潘朵拉一些有關餐桌上的禮儀——首要的是，不要學賴皮的吃相！

 Kids, it's ready!

Don't talk with your mouth full. Use a napkin to wipe your mouth.

Don't chew with your mouth open. Eat slowly!

Drink slowly, taking small sips.

Be careful not to spill your glass. Always remember to say "please" and "thank you". Don't leave any food on your plate.

⭐ 試着用英語説出以下的句子。

1. 嘴裏滿是食物時，不要説話。

2. 不要張大嘴巴咀嚼食物。

答案：1. Don't talk with your mouth full. 2. Don't chew with your mouth open.

DO YOU REMEMBER?
你還記得嗎？

潘朵拉和班哲文很想知道賴皮、柏蒂和我在孩童時期是怎樣度過我們的假期的，你也想知道嗎？一起來看看吧！

Trappola: Do you remember the time when Aunt Lippa took us to the seaside?
Geronimo: Yes, I remember!

Geronimo: One day I built a beautiful sandcastle!
Trappola: Yes, I remember!

Geronimo: One summer we went on holiday to England to learn English!

Trappola: I spent all summer in the mountains. What a wonderful holiday!

 試着用英語説出：「我整個夏天都是在山裏度過的。」

答案： I spent all summer in the mountains.

How did you spend your holidays when you were little?

I toured round Mouse Island in a camper, with Mum and Dad once.

I went on holiday on my bicycle once.

When I was a kid, I spent the summer on a canal boat once.

Did you have fun, Uncle G?

I did... a lot!

 試着用英語説出：「你玩得開心嗎？」

答案：Did you have fun?

A POSTCARD TO...
寄一張明信片給……

我們在鼠爪灣玩得真開心！可是菲這次不能跟我們一起來，於是班哲文提議給菲姑姐寄一張明信片，這主意多好啊！

Shall we send a postcard to Aunt Tea?

What a good idea... but how?

Look, you write the address...

... you write a message and you sign it!

Sgraffignolo Harbour

Greetings from

stamp

Benjamin

Pandora

Geronimo

Patty

Trappola

To our dear Tea Stilton
2, Borgoratto Street
13131 Topazia
Mouse Island

address

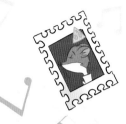

A SONG FOR YOU!

Track 2

A Postcard

I love writing postcards,
I love sending greetings,
I always write to my aunt
when I am on holiday.
Put a stamp on your mail
and post it,
postcards and letters
travel quickly,
it's always nice to get a postcard
from someone you love.

I love writing letters
to my best friend.
He lives far away
but letters arrive everywhere!
Put a stamp on your mail
and post it,
postcards and letters
travel quickly,
it's always nice to
get a postcard
from someone you love.
I love writing letters
to my best friend.
He lives far away
but letters arrive everywhere!

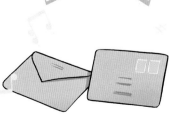

〈一次輕鬆的交通擠塞事件〉

潘朵拉：我們終於可以去度假啦！我已等不及要到海裏游泳了！

班哲文：叔叔，我們什麼時候可以到達臭味港？

謝利連摩：如果不塞車的話，我們一小時內便會到達。

賴皮：謝利連摩，我已提你多少年……

賴皮：當我們在高速公路上行駛時，
不要預報交通情況。

〔收音機〕……嘟嘟嘟……一架運載香蕉
的貨車翻側，情況並不嚴重，但是……
司機甲：我們至少在四小時內不能移動！
司機乙：他們要把所有香蕉從馬路上搬走
啊！

謝利連摩：所有汽車都把引擎關掉了。
我們也應下車吧。

謝利連摩：啊！這裏燙得像着火！
老鼠甲：我的乳酪呀！被困在袋
子裏四小時，一定會變質的！
賴皮：嗯……我有一個好
主意！

賴皮：煙烤乳酪！班哲文，你要一些嘗嘗嗎？

柏蒂：好極了！加些水果就更完美了。
老鼠乙：水果？我有很多呀！

老鼠乙：你喜歡哪一種水果？桃子、西瓜，還是菠蘿？

與此同時……

老鼠丙：我要把這些水運去哪裏？
賴皮：那邊，給那隻正在把游泳池充氣的男鼠。

五分鐘後……
謝利連摩：嗨，聽着！
〔收音機〕……嘟嘟嘟……馬路現在解封了，所有汽車可以在幾分鐘內恢復行駛。
班哲文、潘朵拉：噢，不！

柏蒂：你們説「不」是什麼意思？別忘記我們正在去度假啊！
班哲文：但我們已覺得像在度假了。

謝利連摩：你説得對。在任何地方都可以度假，只要你遇到好人，就算是在高速公路遇上交通擠塞也可以。

TEST 小測驗

⭐ 1. 用英語説出下面的詞彙。

> **(a)** 帳篷 　　　**(b)** 牀墊 　　　**(c)** 睡袋 　　　**(d)** 手電筒

⭐ 2. 用英語説出下面的句子。

> **(a)** 你昨晚睡得着嗎？
> Did ... ... last ... ?
> **(b)** 我根本沒睡着！
> I ... ... at all!

⭐ 3. 讀出下面的詞彙，並用中文説出它們的意思。

> **(a)** twin room
> **(b)** room with the sea view
> **(c)** double room
> **(d)** single room

⭐ 4. 把下面的字詞重新排好次序，組成一句意思完整的句子，然後讀出來。

> The swimming pool 　 the garden 　 is just 　 across

⭐ 5. 用英語説出下面的詞彙。

> **(a)** 明信片 　　　**(b)** 地址 　　　**(c)** 郵票

DICTIONARY 詞典

A

address　地址

at last　最後

B

bananas　香蕉

barbecue　燒烤

bathroom　浴室

beauty centre　美容中心

bicycle　單車

break out　突然發生

breakfast　早餐

bungalow　平房

burning　着火

C

camp bed　帆布牀

camper　露營車

camping stove

露營專用煮食爐

campsite　營地

cheese　乳酪

chew　咀嚼

clues　線索

comics　漫畫

convinced　説服

cooler bag　冷藏袋

cooler box　冷藏箱

D

dinner　晚餐

dining room　飯廳

double room
　有一張雙人牀的雙人房

E

engines　引擎
England　英國
English　英文

F

facilities　設施
food　食物
forecasts　預報
forget　忘記
friends　朋友
fruit　水果
full　滿

G

games room　遊戲室
garden　花園
go back　回去

go off　變質
greetings　問候
grilled fish　烤魚
group leader　組長

H

holiday　假期
hotel　酒店

I

in the end　最後
inflating　使充氣
information desk　詢問處

K

keys　鎖匙（普：鑰匙）

L

lasagne　闊條麵（普：寬條麵）
learn　學習
lift　升降機

look for　找尋

lorry　貨車

lunch　午餐

M

mattress　牀墊

motorway　高速公路

mountains　山

N

napkin　餐巾

O

organise　安排

P

parents　父母

pasta　意大利粉

peaches　桃子

perfect　完美

picnic　野餐

pineapples　菠蘿

plate　碟子

plenty　很多

porter　雜工

postcard　明信片

R

reception　接待處

relaxing　輕鬆的

remember　記得

river　河

room with the sea view
　　海景套房

S

sandcastle　沙堡壘

seaside　海邊

send　寄

serious　嚴重

sign　簽名

single room　單人房

sleep 睡覺

sleeping bag 睡袋

stamp 郵票

storm 暴風雨

suggests 提議

summer 夏天

sunrise 日出

swim 游泳

swimming pool 游泳池

switch off 關掉

T

tent 帳篷

toilets 廁所

tomato sauce 番茄醬

torch 手電筒

traffic jam 交通擠塞

（普：交通堵塞）

treasure 寶藏

twin room

有兩張單人牀的雙人房

U

unusual 獨特的

W

waiter 侍應

（普：服務員）

waitress 女侍應

（普：女服務員）

walk 散步

watermelons 西瓜

woods 樹林

worry 擔心

Y

yesterday 昨天

看在一千塊莫澤雷勒乳酪的份上，你學得開心嗎？很開心，對不對？好極了！跟你一起跳舞唱歌我也很開心！我等着你下次繼續跟班哲文和潘朵拉一起玩一起學英語呀。現在要說再見了，當然是用英語說啦！

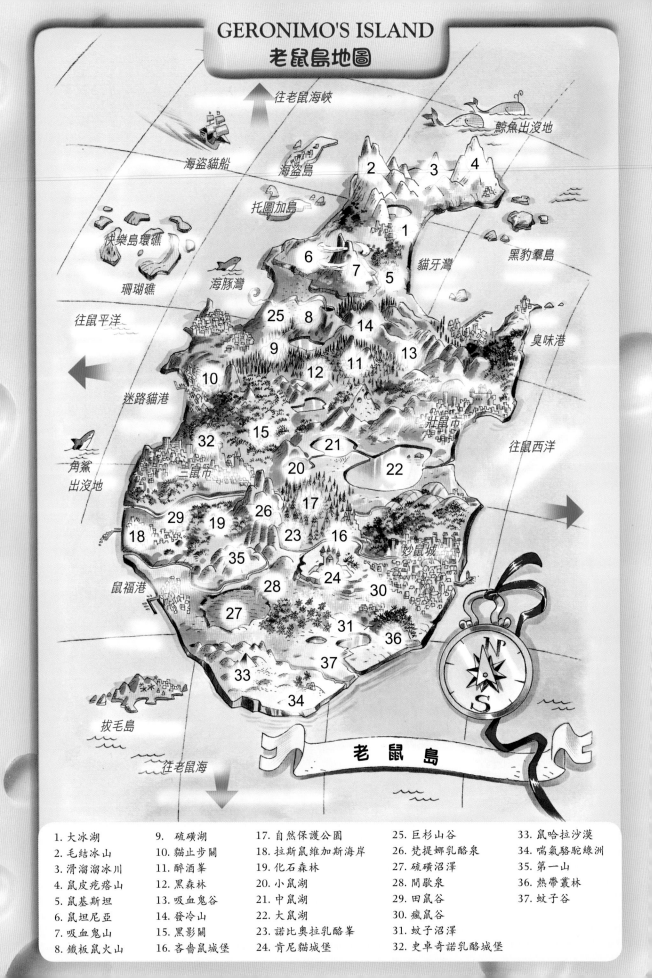

GERONIMO'S ISLAND
老鼠島地圖

往老鼠海峽

鯨魚出沒地

海盜貓船　　海盜島

托圖加島

快樂島環礁

珊瑚礁　　海豚灣

往鼠平洋

貓牙灣

黑豹羣島

臭味港

迷路貓港

往鼠西洋

角鯊
出沒地

壯鼠市

三鼠市

砂鼠城

鼠福港

老鼠島

往老鼠海

拔毛島

1. 大冰湖
2. 毛結冰山
3. 滑溜溜冰川
4. 鼠皮疙瘩山
5. 鼠基斯坦
6. 鼠坦尼亞
7. 吸血鬼山
8. 鐵板鼠火山

9. 硫磺湖
10. 貓止步關
11. 醉酒峯
12. 黑森林
13. 吸血鬼谷
14. 發冷山
15. 黑影關
16. 客魯鼠城堡

17. 自然保護公園
18. 拉斯鼠維加斯海岸
19. 化石森林
20. 小鼠湖
21. 中鼠湖
22. 大鼠湖
23. 諾比奧拉乳酪峯
24. 肯尼貓城堡

25. 巨杉山谷
26. 梵提娜乳酪泉
27. 硫磺沼澤
28. 間歇泉
29. 田鼠谷
30. 瘋鼠谷
31. 蚊子沼澤
32. 史卓奇諾乳酪城堡

33. 鼠哈拉沙漠
34. 喘氣駱駝綠洲
35. 第一山
36. 熱帶叢林
37. 蚊子谷

Geronimo Stilton

EXERCISE BOOK
練習冊

想知道自己對 ON HOLIDAY 掌握了多少，
趕快打開後面的練習完成它吧！

ENGLISH!

26 ON HOLIDAY 去度假

AT THE CAMPSITE
在營地上

★ 謝利連摩他們帶了很多物品去露營。你知道這些物品的英文名稱嗎？選出代表答案的英文字母填在空格內。

A. sleeping bag   B. tent   C. torch
D. mattress   E. camp bed   F. camping stove

I REMEMBER...
我記得……

★ 柏蒂跟大家分享她以前去露營的經歷。從下面選出適當的字詞填在橫線上，完成柏蒂的話。

treasure hunt	treasure	clues
comics	camp	

1. When I was a little girl, I used to come here to _____ .

2. I remember our group leader organised a _____ once.

3. We started to look for the _____ .

4. In the end we found the _____ !

5. It was a pile of _____ .

WHAT FUN! 真好玩！

⭐ 根據圖畫，選出適當的句子，把代表答案的英文字母填在空格內，然後讀出句子。

A. Patty organises a trip to the river.

B. Pandora suggests a walk in the woods.

C. A storm breaks out and everybody has to go back!

1.

2.
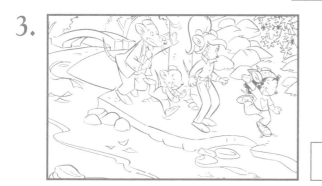

3.

THE SEASIDE HOLIDAY
到海邊度假

⭐ 謝利連摩他們住在近海邊的一間酒店裏。你知道下面這些與酒店有關的英文詞彙的意思嗎？把它們與相配的中文詞彙用線連起來。

1. single room ● ● 女侍應

2. twin room ● ● 接待處

3. double room ● ● 詢問處

4. waitress ● ● 有兩張單人牀的雙人房

5. waiter ● ● 海景套房

6. lift ● ● 侍應

7. reception ● ● 有一張雙人牀的雙人房

8. information desk ● ● 單人房

9. room with the sea view ● ● 升降機

KIDS, IT'S READY!
孩子們，準備好了！

⭐ 根據圖畫，從下面選出適當的句子寫在橫線上，然後讀出句子。

Don't chew with
your mouth open.

Be careful not to
spill your glass.

Drink slowly,
taking small sips.

Don't talk with
your mouth full.

1.

_____

_____

2.

_____

_____

3.

_____

_____

4.

_____

_____

DO YOU REMEMBER?
你還記得嗎？

★ 賴皮和謝利連摩談起他們小時候去度假的有趣事，從下面選出適當的字詞填在橫線上，完成他們的對話。

| remember | went | spent | built |

1.

Do you remember...

Yes, I _____ !

2.

One day I _____ a beautiful sandcastle!

3.

One summer we _____ on holiday to England to learn English!

4.

I _____ all summer in the mountains!

6

A POSTCARD TO...
寄一張明信片給……

⭐ 試想像一下，你去了旅行，你想寄一張明信片給你的一位朋友或親戚問候一下。參考班哲文他們寄給菲的明信片，完成下面的明信片吧！

Sgraffignolo Harbour

Greetings from

Benjamin   **Pandora**

Geronimo

Patty   *Trappola*

To our dear Tea Stilton
2, Borgoratto Street
13131 Topazia
Mouse Island

ANSWERS 答案

TEST 小測驗

1. (a) tent   (b) mattress   (c) sleeping bag   (d) torch
2. (a) Did <u>you</u> <u>sleep</u> last <u>night</u>?   (b) I <u>didn't</u> <u>sleep</u> at all!
3. (a) 有兩張單人牀的雙人房   (b) 海景套房   (c) 有一張雙人牀的雙人房   (d) 單人房
4. The swimming pool is just across the garden.
5. (a) postcard   (b) address   (c) stamp

EXERCISE BOOK 練習冊

P.1

P.2

1. camp   2. treasure hunt
3. clues   4. treasure   5. comics

P.3

1. C   2. B   3. A

P.4

1. single room 單人房   2. twin room 有兩張單人牀的雙人房
3. double room 有一張雙人牀的雙人房   4. waitress 女侍應   5. waiter 侍應   6. lift 升降機
7. reception 接待處   8. information desk 詢問處   9. room with the sea view 海景套房

P.5

1. Don't talk with your mouth full.   2. Don't chew with your mouth open.
3. Drink slowly, taking small sips.   4. Be careful not to spill your glass.

P.6

1. remember   2. built   3. went   4. spent

P.7

自由發揮，答案合理便可。